To my fellow Big Trees Campers, in honor of our many searches for spring
—D. S.

For LJ and Wes: here's to many years of searching for new adventures together
—S. H.

Farrar Straus Giroux Books for Young Readers
An imprint of Macmillan Publishing Group, LLC
120 Broadway, New York, NY 10271 • mackids.com

Text copyright © 2024 by Dashka Slater
Illustrations copyright © 2024 by Sydney Hanson
All rights reserved

Our books may be purchased in bulk for promotional, educational, or business use.
Please contact your local bookseller or the Macmillan Corporate and Premium Sales Department
at (800) 221-7945 ext. 5442 or by email at MacmillanSpecialMarkets@macmillan.com.

Library of Congress Cataloging-in-Publication Data is available.

First edition, 2024
Book design by Asher Caswell
Color separations by Embassy Graphics
Printed in China by RR Donnelley Asia Printing Solutions Ltd., Dongguan City, Guangdong Province

ISBN 978-0-374-31427-9
1 3 5 7 9 10 8 6 4 2

Escargot
AND THE SEARCH FOR SPRING

STORY BY Dashka Slater

PICTURES BY Sydney Hanson

FARRAR STRAUS GIROUX · NEW YORK

Bonjour! I was hoping you would open this book!
You are looking very nice today.
Perhaps you would say the same about me?
Of course, a beautiful French snail like Escargot looks nice every day!
But . . .
do you think I seem a little pale?

Does it seem like my eyes are not so bright?
Do my tentacles look droopy?
Perhaps my trail isn't quite as shimmery as before?
I was afraid of this.

It has been a long winter,
and Escargot is suffering from *ennui*,
which is the feeling you have
when you are bored with everything.

I am tired of making snow angels
and snow snails
and wearing cozy sweaters.

I am even tired of
hot chocolate!

But now, I must tell you something terrible.
So terrible, you might faint!
I am fainting just thinking about it.
Perhaps you can fan me so I recover.

Okay, I will tell you the terrible thing:
Escargot is trapped!
There is an enormous snowbank blocking the front door!

I have made a decision.
I will dig through the enormous snowbank
and go out into the world to look for signs of spring.
You should come!

While we are digging through the snow, we can talk.
Tell me, what do you do when you are suffering from *ennui*?

Do you read an interesting book?

Invent an elegant new dance?

Change the style of your tentacles?

Sometimes it helps to kiss a snail,
but only if you want to.

I am just trying to help!

One way to overcome *ennui*
is to have an amusing conversation.
Do you know any good jokes?
I will tell one first.
Knock knock!
   (Now you must say "Who's there?")
Lettuce!
   (You say "Lettuce who?")
Lettuce begin our search for spring!

If you do not know any jokes, you can share an interesting fact.
Did you know that snails can sleep for three years? *C'est vrai!*
A snail is a world-champion sleeper!

Is it just me, or is that snowbank following us?

Oh là là! It is not a snowbank! It is a bunny rabbit!
What is a bunny rabbit doing in our book?
We were having a nice time, just the two of us, *n'est-ce pas?*
We don't need any bunny rabbits.

You probably think the bunny rabbit is adorable.
More adorable than a French snail
who is suffering from a terrible case of *ennui*.
Perhaps you want to tell jokes with this bunny rabbit
and share facts about long bunny ears and fluffy bunny tails
and how high a bunny can hop.

I do not find these facts at all interesting.
But you can stay here if you like.
I will continue on alone.

Excusez-moi, Bunny Rabbit. I said I was continuing on *alone*! I am very busy searching for spring and do not have time to be bothered by bunny rabbits.

If you do not leave my book *tout de suite*,
I will be forced to make a fierce face at you.

This is your final warning, Bunny Rabbit.
I am now going into my shell.
I expect you to be gone when I come out.

Quoi?! The bunny rabbit is still here? C'*est inacceptable!*
This is NOT a BUNNY BOOK.
There are plenty of *other* books for bunny rabbits to go hopping around in.
If anyone is going to be hopping around in *this* book, it will be me.

You don't believe that Escargot can hop?

Fine, the bunny and I will have a contest.
You can be the judge.
Whoever hops the highest can have the whole book to themselves.
We will hop on the count of three.
Un, deux, trois, sautez!

Did you see my jump?
It was so fast, you might have missed it.
I hopped all the way to the moon!
Which was full of . . . moony things . . .
like moonbeams and moon rocks and
moon . . . salads.
I would have brought some back
but I had to get here before the rabbit . . .

who seems to have hopped right out of the book.

I am the winner!

Oh. Merci.

It is possible that I don't have *ennui* after all.
Maybe I was just hungry.
A hungry snail is a sad snail.
And also . . . a rude snail.

Perhaps the bunny rabbit would like to
stay in my book after all?

The sun is shining. The birds are singing.
The snow is melting.
And look—flowers!
The first sign of spring.

Let us eat them together.
Bon appetit!